STAGE FRIGHTS

Vol. 1
A COLLECTION OF SHORT HORROR PLAYS

GHOST LIGHT PUBLICATIONS

STAGE FRIGHTS

© 2024. All rights reserved.

The works within this book are fully protected under the copyright laws of the USA. All rights, including without limitation professional/amateur stage rights, motion picture, recitation, lecturing, public reading, radio broadcasting, television, video or sound recording, all other forms of mechanical, electronic and digital reproduction, transmission and distribution, such as CD, DVD, the Internet, private and file-sharing networks, information storage and retrieval systems, photocopying, and the rights of translation into foreign languages are strictly reserved.

No professional or nonprofessional performance of any plays may be given without contacting the authors. For production rights inquiries, please contact info@ghostlightpubs.com to get connected with the playwrights.

Cover & Book Design: Jonathan Cook
First Edition: November 2024
ISBN: 978-1-964045-06-1

STAGE FRIGHTS
Vol. 1

If you like horror, you're in the right place.
If you like theatre, you're in the right place.
If you like horror theatre, you just hit the jackpot.

Table of Contents

CLIP CLOP

By Greg Mandryk

A nighttime run turns into a race for survival.

CHARACTERS

NARRATOR ONE
Any gender. Any age.

NARRATOR TWO
Any gender. Any age.

JOGGER
The jogger.

SETTING

Late at night on a dark country road.

***

The stage is dimly lit. The Narrators One and Two take their positions DSL. One has a flashlight, which she holds under her face in the fashion of a campfire ghost story. Two has a small table, upon which is set a pair of cups along with various other instruments to be used for making sound effects. Whenever Two speaks, One holds her flashlight under her face.

ONE. Nighttime. A country road. The world was all black tar and chalk dust under the pale moon. The sun had set and the day's heat had been subdued. It was an absolutely perfect night… for a run. *(The Jogger appears. He takes his place center stage and runs in place.)* But the woods can be a dangerous place. And the darkness makes them doubly so. He had been warned. His mother often told him…

TWO. "Don't go running at night, dear. It isn't safe."

ONE. A pearl of wisdom from a worrisome mother.

TWO. "You can't see where you're going. You might trip and break your ankle. And then where would you be?"

ONE. But there was something in the woman's expression that warned of darker, more insidious threats. Perils that can only exist in the imagination of an overly protective mother.

TWO. "Just promise me you'll be careful."

ONE. And he had listened. When he was younger. But now…

JOGGER. *(Breathes deeply.)* Ahhh!

ONE. The air was brisk. It cooled him as he glided over the smooth pavement, his legs carrying him effortlessly. His heartbeat was steady, his breathing unlabored. Years of discipline had paid off. The once torturous exercise had become a source of primal enjoyment. He paused under a streetlamp. *(The Jogger stops running. A spot illuminates him. He checks his pulse while examining the road ahead.)* Up ahead, he could see headlights. A car was approaching. Speeding, definitely. Not minding the lines too well.

JOGGER. Drunk? Stupid?

ONE. The car drew closer. Should he wait in the light where he could be seen? Maybe get off the road completely?

JOGGER. Screw it. *(He continues running. The light fades.)*

ONE. If it was his fate to be roadkill, so be it.

TWO. "It's dangerous, Sweetie."

JOGGER. Thanks, Mom.

ONE. The headlights began to illuminate the area surrounding him. As the car came closer, the light filtering through the trees, the grass, every tiny pebble lent a kaleidoscopic effect to the landscape. The car came closer. *(A headlight effect illuminates the Jogger. Two creates the Doppler sound effect of the car approaching.)*

JOGGER. Jesus. Easy on the brights!

ONE. The car was almost on top of him now, the lights two angry eyes bearing down on him. *(The headlight goes out. Jogger watches as car passes.)*

TWO. *(As an obnoxious teenager.)* "Keep running, numb nuts! Whoo!"

JOGGER. *(Facing forward again.)* Asshats.

ONE. He didn't think much of the local youth. Rich kids, unholy terrors...

JOGGER. Future world leaders.

ONE. The woodland nightscape returned to its ephemeral tranquility. The chirping of insects accompanied the rhythm of his footfalls as he continued on into the night. *(Music begins to play quietly.)* Music. Very faint. And the indistinct buzz of human voices.

JOGGER. Someone's having a party.

ONE. And then came the barbecue smell. Charcoal and meat blending together into a sweet, carnal perfume.

JOGGER. God, that smells good.

ONE. Even at his most health conscious, he could never say no to a good steak. It was difficult to tell which direction the smell and the noise were coming from. It seemed close. Not that he had any intention of- *(The sound of bushes shaking.)* Something lurched onto the road beside him. A deer? No. He only caught a glimpse as he strode past it, but it appeared to be a person. And then… *(Narrator Two makes the clip clop noise. It is the sound of footsteps following the Jogger. It rises and fades as needed underneath the dialogue.)*

ONE. It was behind him.

JOGGER. What the hell? *(Clip clop clip clop.)*

ONE. Following.

JOGGER. Great. A pacer.

ONE. "Pacer". A term he'd coined. During his many jogs through suburbia, children would see him running and decide…

JOGGER. *(Disgustedly.)* Yay.

TWO. *(A child.)* "Let's have a race!"

ONE. And try to outrun him.

JOGGER. Moron.

ONE. In the late-night hours, drunks sometimes did this, too. Exactly what he had here… *(Clip clop clip clop.)* By the sound of it.

JOGGER. *(To himself.)* Okay. Let's race.

ONE. Pushing himself past his normal pace, he sped onward. He hadn't seen his short-lived companion very well. Just a dark shape emerging from a collection of shadows in his peripheral vision. He could turn to get a better look, but not without breaking his stride. And he felt that a snubbing was in order.

JOGGER. *(Twangy accent; to himself.)* Eat muh dust! *(Clip clop clip clop clip clop.)*

ONE. Acknowledgement would only encourage him. Of course, it wasn't entirely impossible that his pursuer meant him harm.

JOGGER. *(Considers.)* Naw.

ONE. He had no money, no wallet. Only the key to a car that was parked three miles away. If he was willing to wear himself out for that…

JOGGER. Come n' get it.

ONE. But still… *(Clip clop clip clop.)* He was keeping pace considerably well, for a drunk. Judging by the sound, he--

TWO. *(As Mom.)* Or she.

ONE. --was only a dozen paces behind. And not giving up.

JOGGER. It's alca-sauras triathletus, the fastest of the drunken dinosaurs.

ONE. He wasn't worried. Not yet. The pacer was running as though one leg were six inches shorter than the other. He wouldn't… he couldn't last much longer. And yet… *(Clip clop clip clop clip clop.)* Was it getting closer? Hard to believe and yet he seemed to be gaining. Their footfalls were beginning to match, the lighter blended in with his own, but the heavier swallowed his every time he set his right foot down.

JOGGER. No way he's running me down. No way.

ONE. He had been running faster than his usual pace. The exertion was beginning to sap his stamina. He wanted to give up this little game, turn around and face his pursuer. But a tiny voice inside his head told him…

TWO. "Don't… turn around." *(Clip clop clip clop.)*

ONE. He began to entertain the notion that this person might very well be a deranged killer. Curiosity was beginning to play its hand. An unfamiliar voice spoke inside his head.

TWO. "Know what? Turn around. Who knows what you might see."

JOGGER. Nope.

ONE. He kept running. He decided that if he…

TWO. *(As Mom.)* "Or it…"

ONE. Fell behind, he'd take a peek. But, as long as it was only a few paces behind…

JOGGER. I do not break stride.

ONE. But just then… *(The clip clop noise stops.)* It was over.

JOGGER. *(Still running but looking over his shoulder.)* That's it?

ONE. He came to a stop under a streetlight. *(Light shines down on Jogger. He stops running.)* He looked behind him. There was only the harsh light surrounding him and the utter blackness beyond. He waited for his eyes to adjust. He could make out a few details: the road, the shoulder…. But there was no one to be seen. It suddenly unnerved him that his pursuer, concealed behind a tree would have no problem seeing him, and worse, seeing that he had stopped. He continued running. *(Jogger resumes running. The street light goes out.)* His trot was steady, but keeping ahead of the limping bogeyman cost him some of his steam. It would be a long run home. *(Jogger looks over his shoulder.)* The light was receding behind him. He half-expected to see a tired drunk staggering into the light. But none appeared.

JOGGER. Still… creepy.

ONE. He continued onward. And again, the night was still. Still, but not serene. There was a latent menace lurking just out of sight. He just wanted to be home. He began to plot the quickest route to his car. Maybe he'd get takeout… *(The sound of twigs snapping and leaves rustling violently.*

Jogger reacts.) A noise from above. *(A crashing sound.)* Something heavy landing behind him. He almost stopped, turned to see what it was. But then… *(Clip clop clip clop clip clop.)* It wasn't human. It couldn't be. What could drop twenty feet onto solid pavement and immediately break into a run?

TWO. "You really shouldn't go running at night."

ONE. It had stopped chasing him. Why?

JOGGER. Oh crap! Oh crap, oh crap, oh crap!

ONE. The light! It wouldn't go into the light! *(Clip clop clip clop clip clop.)* He didn't want to know what it was. Curiosity could go kill some other damn cat. He just wanted to run.

JOGGER. Just keep going. Right, left, right, left…

ONE. There would be another light up ahead. If he could just keep up his pace. *(Clip clop clip clop.)* It was unbearably close now. He could hear its raspy breathing. He could smell the putrid stench of rotten meat.

JOGGER. What the hell does it want with me?

ONE. But he knew. He had known it when he was three years old, and his parents left him in his room at night with nothing but the darkness and the things that lurked within it. He knew then of sickly skinned bogies with gnarled teeth and clacking talons dwelling beneath his bed in murderous contemplation, hungrily waiting for a tender foot to dangle within their reach.

JOGGER. Oh, God!

ONE. The road curved ahead, and he could see the next streetlamp, a flat disk of light on the road.

JOGGER. Base! Gotta make it to base!

ONE. There was a tug at the back of his shirt, the feeling of a thorn snagging the fabric. He found the strength to run faster.

JOGGER. Come on! Rightleftrightleftrightleft! *(Clipclop clipclopclipclop!)*

TWO. "If I've taught you anything in your miserable life, it's that you shouldn't go running at night!!"

ONE. He was past his normal threshold of fatigue. The air he breathed seemed devoid of oxygen. He felt pains he hadn't experienced since he first took up running years ago: the stabbing in his ribs, the sloshing of his intestines… But the light was nearer. He was almost under it. If he could just push a little harder… *(The clip clop noise stops abruptly.)* And then it stopped. The breathing, the footsteps. The chase was over. *(Light cascades over the Jogger. He stops. He bends over, putting his hands over his knees and tries to catch his breath.)* His breath burned in the back of his throat. His legs were rubbery. It was an effort to not simply collapse. He looked behind him. *(He does.)* Nothing. The road was clear for as far as he could see. There was nothing there. Was it ever there?

JOGGER. That wasn't my goddam imagination! Something was after me. I could hear it. Christ, I could smell it!

ONE. But it wasn't there now. It was hiding, he knew. Like the first time.

JOGGER. The trees. It's in the trees.

ONE. Of course, he never really saw it.

JOGGER. No, sir. Never saw a thing. Just a little something out of the corner of my eye. Could have been anything.

ONE. His mind was eager to believe he'd imagined the whole thing. The light helped. Under the streetlamp. There was pavement, grass, bushes… Real things that were part of the real world. And there were no monsters in the real world. Maybe there was no real danger. Maybe he could make it…

JOGGER. Oh, hell no. Staying right here. A car will come along. I'll just tell them I twisted my ankle. No need to mention any tree-hopping boogie men. I'll wait until dawn if I have to. *(Shouting.)* You hear that? I'm waiting right here! *(Jogger sits.)*

ONE. Silence. *(Pause.)* But then… *(The sound of something small passing through the trees. A fist-sized rock lands on the stage.)*

JOGGER. Throwing stuff at me? Fine. Throw away. I'm not leaving the light.

ONE. And then another. *(The sound of a rock passing through the trees again, followed by the sound of metal being struck.)* And he realized… it wasn't aiming at him.

JOGGER. *(Looking up at streetlamp.)* Oh god. *(Another rock passes through the trees. It is followed by the sound of breaking glass. The light goes out. There is a brief pause before the clip clop sound resumes. It is slower now. The thing is walking. The Jogger sits frozen. The thing stops. Two makes the sound of the thing exhaling.)*

JOGGER. *(Weakly.)* Mother. *(Lights out.)*

END OF PLAY

FIRST SHIFT

by Leah Philbin

A new hire at a security job soon realizes that this is no ordinary workplace.

CHARACTERS

KAI
Male or female, twenties, an American accent.

TOD
Male or female, fifties - sixties, RP British accent.

BOWLER HAT MAN
Male or female, any age. Creepy with a menacing laugh.

GOOGLE MAPS
Voice heard from phone (or offstage)

SETTING

Derelict building.

NOTES

This play can be performed as elaborate or as bare as the director seems fit. Being creative with sound and lighting effects is encouraged.

Feel free to adjust pronouns based on your casting choices.

***

At rise, Kai Reynolds is following his phone GPS to reach the location of his new job.

GOOGLE MAPS. Turn left, and you will reach your destination.

KAI. What? That can't be right.

GOOGLE MAPS. You have reached your destination.

KAI. This place looks derelict! *(He bangs on the metal door at the entrance of the building, which is then followed by an echo.)* Hello? Brian? *(He bangs on the door again, before pushing it open. It creaks, followed by a loud slam as it closes behind him.)* Brian, are you there? *(He walks around the room, looking for Brian. He then sees Tod.)* There you are! Hello.

TOD. *(Lackluster.)* Hi.

KAI. I'm Kai.

TOD. *(Disinterested.)* Hello, Kai.

KAI. Erm… I'm new here.

TOD. I see.

KAI. Are you Brian?

TOD. No. I'm Tod.

KAI. Nice to meet you, Tod! *(Silence.)* Not much of a conversationalist, eh?

TOD. Life is short. Small talk only makes it shorter.

KAI. *(Laughing before stopping himself.)* Fair enough, but the problem is… I'm new.

TOD. So you said.

KAI. And, because it's my first day, I was supposed to meet Brian here, so he could train me up. They said that his shift would start at the same time as mine, so he could do my induction.

TOD. Who told you that? Brian isn't even working today!

KAI. Hang on, let me check my phone. *(He looks at his phone and reads.)* Brenda Davies, from Crystal Lake recruitment agency. She emailed me.

TOD. Oh, did she now? And did Brenda Davies warn you about the high staff turnover we have here?

KAI. Erm… She didn't.

TOD. Well, I'm sure you'll find out soon enough. Have you ever worked as a security guard before?

KAI. No…

TOD. *(Sighing, irritated.)* For God's sake…

KAI. Erm… I'm a kickboxer?

TOD. We just need you to monitor the building, walk around regularly to check for squatters and the like, and make sure people don't break in. None of that involves kicking people.

KAI . But we may need to throw people out if they break in, to protect the building-

TOD. *(Interrupting.)* Trust me, it's the people who break in that need protecting.

KAI. I don't understand.

TOD. Tell you what, let me show you around. *(They walk around the building.)* Kai, did anyone explain the ten rules?

KAI. The rules for working here? Yes, Brenda sent them with the contract.

TOD. They are very important. Have you memorised them?

KAI. No, erm… I haven't read them yet.

TOD. Where the hell did they find you?

KAI. Linked In…

TOD. Well, fortunately for you, I have a spare copy. Hang on. *(He hands Kai the rules written on a crumbled paper.)* Learn these, they'll keep you safe.

KAI. Okay…

TOD. It's very important you understand that this is a highly unique building. Things are not as they seem.

KAI. I don't follow?

TOD. Put it this way; did you never wonder why a basic security job paid so well?

KAI. I didn't want to push my luck by asking. It was this or McDonalds.

TOD. Many strange and unexplainable things happen here, and it can be dangerous. You might want to read those rules.

KAI. Rule One: do not drink the tap water. You may wash your hands, providing the water isn't purple or red. *(He pauses, before laughing.)* Red water stings, purple water will melt away your skin.

TOD. What's so funny?

KAI. This! Obviously, it's a joke.

TOD. You try telling that to the last lad Brenda sent. He didn't even make it past the first day. *(He turns on the taps. Sound of creaky pipes and running water.)*

KAI. I see, well… What the hell?

TOD. What?

KAI. The water! It's purple!

TOD. Which means?

KAI. Sorry?

TOD. *(Exasperated.)* The rule!

KAI. Oh! Purple is bad. How did you do that? Is this some kind of optical illusion? Creative first-day hazing? *(Tod runs off the taps.)*

TOD. Just don't forget to check the color of the water before you wash your hands.

KAI. *(Amused; Skeptical)* Tell you what - I'll just avoid the taps altogether. I have hand sanitiser! *(Tod sighs. They continue to walk to an elevator. Sound of elevator bell.)* Rule two: if you hear screaming coming from the seventh floor, enter the elevator car, press the seventh-floor button, then exit immediately. Do not, under any circumstances, stay in the elevator as it reaches the seventh floor. It isn't fair on Mary. Who's Mary?

TOD. Our cleaner. It'll take her hours to scrape you off the walls. Just here is the staff room.

KAI. *(Laughing; Cynical.)* I don't fancy being human wallpaper, I'll give it a miss. *(A scream is heard in the distance.)* What was that?

TOD. What was what?

KAI. The blood curdling scream!

TOD. Oh, I didn't notice. Don't worry, you'll get used to that.

KAI. I'm not sure I want to get used to that! *(Tod opens a door and the sound of buzzing electrical circuits is heard.)*

TOD. This is the boiler room. Do you want to take a look?

KAI. It sounds a bit hazardous in there. I'm worried I might get electrocuted.

TOD. Oh, that'll be the least of your problems. I suggest checking rule number three.

KAI. Okay. Rule three: During a power cut, reset the fuse box in the boiler room. You may use your flashlight, but do not point it at the ceiling and definitely do not look up. Remember – as long as you can't see them, they can't see you. *(There are loud, chaotic, scuttling sounds followed by pipes creaking then a loud smash. Scared, Kai gasps.)*

TOD. *(Amused.)* Listen to them go, the scamps! Just don't shine your light at them and you'll be fine. You'll probably be fine. Possibly.

KAI. I'm starting to have second thoughts about this, Tod. *(Silence.)* Can I ask you something… How long have you worked here?

TOD. Longer than you've been alive.

KAI. *(Exasperated.)* How old do you think I am?

TOD. I don't know… Twelve? Anyway, the stairs are here. In the event of an emergency, never use the lift-

KAI. Why? Because the elevator monster will swallow me whole?

TOD. No, to avoid being trapped inside if the power fails.

KAI. Yeah, that makes sense.

TOD. Speaking of fires… Keep going.

KAI. Rule four… If the fire alarm goes off between one AM and two AM, ignore it. They're just trying to catch you out. *(Panicked.)* Who is trying to catch me out?

TOD. And here is a map of the building. There are six floors, plus a basement. *(The sound of a roar can be heard, followed by chains clanking together.)*

KAI. *(Frightened.)* Tod, has anything bad ever happened to you in this building?

TOD. Such as?

KAI. Nothing, forget it.

TOD. Don't worry, I will. You're not very memorable. Anyway, here are some of the old warehouse entrances. Just keep an eye on them, and always follow rule five.

KAI. Rule five: when visiting the warehouses, you must turn on the overhead lights before you enter. They can move a lot faster than you in the dark. What moves faster? Tod?

TOD. It might be clearer if I open the door. *(He opens the door. There is the sound of wailing and inhuman screams. Tod then slams the door shut and the noises stop.)*

KAI. Tod, I'm worried! This sounds really bad… Inhuman, even! I'm not sure--

TOD. *(Interrupting; Upbeat.)* And over here is the staff

kitchen – Julia made a birthday cake! Help yourself.

KAI. But Tod--

TOD. Wait! You're not allergic to nuts, are you?

KAI. Erm… No.

TOD. You'll be fine, then. Julia has a tendency to slip macadamias in there, they look suspiciously like chocolate chips. Such disappointment. Moving on… *(A man in a bowler hat approaches them from behind. He has a menacing, evil laugh as he walks. Kai panics without turning around.)* Quick bit of advice; might be best if you look down and keep reading.

KAI. Okay. Rule six – if you cross paths with the man in the bowler hat, never look him in the eye, or he'll be the last thing you'll ever see. *(The Bowler Hat Man continues walking past, ignoring them.)*

TOD. To the left, we have the storage room.

KAI. Is it… Erm… Is it safe in here?

TOD. Considering it's just full of boxes, I'd say you'll be fine. Unless you have some kind of aversion to cardboard?

KAI. I meant the building. Is it safe to work here?

TOD. Probably not. *(Tod laughs loudly. Kai joins in, Tod then abruptly stops.)* Just don't veer from the rules. You won't find any sympathy if you ignore the warnings you've been given.

KAI. Got it. Seven: the kitchen on floor two should always be locked. If you ever see the kitchen door open, run… Tod, has anyone ever hurt you? In here?

TOD. A long time ago, but I've moved on. If you look left, you'll see the fire escape and right is the staff room. *(The sound of a chainsaw can be heard in the distance.)*

KAI. *(Panicked.)* What the hell is that?

TOD. Oh, that'll be Marjorie. I'm guessing she's been having a bit of bother with our friends on floor four. The next rule will cover that.

KAI. Number eight: there is a chainsaw in the fourth-floor bathroom. Do not remove it unless essential. If escape is impossible, start up the chainsaw and immediately exit via the stairs, but be warned – their weapons are bigger and sharper. *(The chainsaw can be heard once again, followed by a woman screaming then the sound of a splat.)*

TOD. *(Casually.)* That's a shame, I liked Marjorie.

KAI. What the hell?

TOD. We have stairs to the right, and the basement is just down here. Don't forget about rule nine.

KAI. What? Oh, Rule Nine: At the start of your shift, always leave a nickel on the doormat in reception. If it's still there when you return, urgently evacuate the building. *(Pause; Bewildered)* I'm feeling a bit overwhelmed, Tod.

TOD. Just down these stairs.

KAI. What if I forget? Or get them mixed up? And, erm… What if I don't have a nickel on me, will a dollar suffice?

TOD. And here we have the basement.

KAI. Sweet Jesus, what are the rules down here? Knock three times before entering? Do not turn on the lights on a Tuesday? Throw salt over your shoulder if you hear a loud noise?

TOD. No, Kai. It's just a basement.

KAI. *(Embarrassed.)* Oh… Okay.

TOD. So, are you ready to start?

KAI. Honestly? I don't know. It just sounds like a lot to take in and… Wait. Something's missing.

TOD. What do you mean?

KAI. You said there were ten rules, Tod. There's only nine on here. *(Silence.)*

TOD. Turn over the page. *(Kai gasps in horror. Tod gives*

a sinister laugh, his voice becoming demonic and distorted.)

KAI. *(Horrified.)* Rule ten – do not trust Tod… And do not, under any circumstances, let him take you to the basement.

TOD. *(Distorted, demonic voice.)* You really should have read the rules, Kai.

END OF PLAY

LET THE DEAD BURY THE DEAD

By Mike Brannon

In the midst of a zombie apocalypse, we discover an awful truth - zombies stalk and kill humans because they lack any thoughts or emotions of their own. Eating the flesh allows them to feel again, to relive that slight bit of awareness of what it means to be human again.

Knowing that truth - to what lengths would you be willing to go just to get a final chance to say goodbye?

CHARACTERS

CLINT BAZEMORE
A grizzled veteran zombie survivalist.

EVAN TURNER
A younger, more desperate man trying to survive the zombie apocalypse.

KARIN SOMMERS
Evan's part-time girlfriend.

SETTING

An old, abandoned building, somewhere in what used to be considered "civilization". A heavy metal chair is in the middle of the stage, perhaps against a pillar or a post. A large door is at the back, and a folding chair off to the side.

The near future -- or an alternate version of the present day.

LET THE DEAD BURY THE DEAD by Mike Brannon

***

The stage quiet, empty, the lights low. Lightning crashes, thunder booms - rain falls in sheets from the black sky. From off in the distance, we hear the low, gravelly murmur of the undead as they get closer, and closer...

Suddenly, we hear shouting and cursing. Clint bangs open the upstage door, holding a shotgun in one hand and dragging Evan with the other. He glances around, throws Evan into the room - then turns and securely latches the door.

EVAN. *(Panicking.)* Jesus. Jesus, they're everywhere. Did they follow us here? Did they follow us? Christ, I've never seen a zombie swarm that large. I thought we'd be okay in the RV. I thought we'd be OK. Jesus Christ, they were everywhere.

CLINT. Keep it down.

EVAN. What? Oh, right. Sorry. I'm just a little freaked out. Jesus. I've never seen so many... Jesus. Wait. Hold on. Karin. Where's Karin? What happened to Karin?

CLINT. Who?

EVAN. Karin. My girlfriend Karin. She was in the RV with me. Did she get out? Is she OK? *(He runs up to the door at the back of the room, unlatches it, swings it open, and begins shouting into the storm.)* Karin! Karin!!! *(Clint marches back and grabs Evan by the shoulder, shoving him to the side; Evan stumbles and falls as Clint bolts the door.)*

CLINT. Are you out of your goddamn mind?!?

EVAN. I'm sorry... I'm sorry... it's just that... well, I mean, Karin and I... we've only been together for a few months... but I still can't... I can't believe... *(Evan's voice trails off. Clint sighs and pulls a metal flask out of his pocket.)*

CLINT. It's okay. I understand. Here. Take this flask and drink. *(He hands the flask to Evan, who takes it somewhat reluctantly. Evan sits down in the chair, contemplating.)* If it makes you feel any better... it was too late for her. The swarm was overpowering. There's no way she survived.

EVAN. Sure, but... I mean, if somehow there was a way...

CLINT. There wasn't. Trust me. Drink. *(Evan sags somewhat in his seat, then kicks back a shot and chokes.)*

EVAN. What the hell?!? What is that -- paint thinner?!?

CLINT. Everclear 151. Close enough, I suppose.

EVAN. Holy shit. That's almost pure grain alcohol. That stuff is strong enough to eat a hole through your stomach lining.

CLINT. *(Squinting.)* You got some kind of plan to live forever? *(Evan looks down at the flask, considering.)*

EVAN. I guess not. I guess none of us do. *(Evan sips gingerly from the flask and winces.)* I suppose I should feel lucky to be alive. A few months ago, I was a pharmaceutical rep with a nice cushy office. Now look at me - dirty, bleeding, scared all to shit. And I can't stop shaking. Look here -- I can't stop shaking. Man, when those hulking things lunged through my windows... I thought I was done for. And then you shot that big bald guy with the yellow eyes... and dragged me off to safety...

CLINT. Don't mention it. *(Pause.)* How are you feeling?

EVAN. How am I feeling? I'm feeling good. Well, I'm feeling okay. To be honest with you, I'm think I'm feeling... *(He glances down at the flask and then back at Clint, then down at the flask again. He throws the flask down and leaps from his seat.)* Wait a minute -- what the hell -- did you just poison me?!? Is that your plan? Drug me, torture me, perform some sort of sadistic Edgar Allen Poe, Pit and the Pendulum type shit on me? Is that your plan, you sick son of a bitch? Answer me. Answer me! *(Clint just stares at*

Evan, who eventually calms down.) You're right, you're right -- I'm sorry -- that's crazy talk. I know you didn't poison me. Sorry. Everything that's happened... I guess we all go a little bit crazy sometimes.

CLINT. It's all right. I understand. Times like these... seems like every B-movie horror cliché suddenly applies... *(From the back of the room comes an abrupt banging sound as someone beats on the door.)*

KARIN. *(Offstage.)* Hello? Hello? Is anybody in there?

EVAN. Karin??? *(He leaps to his feet; Clint catches him by the shoulder and spins him around. Karin continues to beat on the door.)*

KARIN. *(Offstage.)* Evan? Evan, is that you? Help me, Evan. I'm bleeding... I don't... I don't know what's happening to me...

EVAN. Let me go! Let me go! She's--

CLINT. She's already gone, son. She's bit, and she'll turn. She's already dead. You have to let her go.

EVAN. *(Still struggling.)* What are you talking about? I hear her. She's alive. She's right there.

CLINT. *(Angrily.)* You want proof? You want to see? Here. *(He tosses Evan to the side, reaches for his shotgun and marches to the back door. He slams back the latch, yanks the door open, and grabs Karin, throwing her into the room. Evan starts to dart towards Karin but freezes when Clint points the shotgun at him.)*

EVAN. What do you think you're doing?

KARIN. *(Shivering.)* Evan... Evan, I don't... I don't think I can... *(She looks down and touches the red blood that is oozing from her stomach. She takes a step toward Evan, and then falls to the ground.)*

EVAN. Karin!!! My God, we have to help her --

CLINT. Don't you dare move a goddamn muscle. You

wanted to watch? Fine. Watch. You need to see what happens.

KARIN. Oh, God, I'm bleeding - I'm bleeding – those things, they bit me, I... I think I'm going to be sick. *(She retches again, then looks up at Evan.)* Evan? Oh, Evan, you're here. Thank God you're here. Thank God you're all right. Help me, Evan. Please. I'm bleeding... I don't feel... *(She collapses. Evan takes a quick step forward but is stopped by Clint's gun. There is a beat as they stare at her.)*

EVAN. Oh my God... is she dead? I think she's dead.

CLINT. Not exactly. Watch. Watch what happens next. *(On the floor, Karin twitches. After a moment, she coughs, then stumbles to her feet, staring at Evan incomprehensively.)*

KARIN. ¿Que esta pasando? ¿Por qué estoy aquí?

EVAN. What? I don't understand.

KARIN. ¿Que esta pasando? ¡Tú no eres mi marido! ¿Qué le pasó a mi familia?

EVAN. I don't speak Spanish. Karin didn't... neither of us spoke Spanish... *(Karin clutches her gut again, spasming. Clint readies his shotgun.)*

CLINT. The herd probably fed upon some Hispanic family somewhere. But just watch. Watch what's happening. *(Karin lurches up again, taking on the voice of an older Southern woman. She turns on Evan reproachfully.)*

KARIN. You shouldn't have gone after them, boy. You should have stayed with us. Let the dead bury the dead, Pa. Let the dead bury the dead...

EVAN. *(Bewildered.)* What?

KARIN. *(Shrieking.)* Let the dead bury the dead! *(Karin shivers, jerks again, and then screams monstrously. Clint cocks his shotgun. Karin turns towards the sound, and he fires, knocking her back into a heap at the other side of the stage.)*

EVAN. *(Screaming.)* Karin!!! *(Evan sinks down to his knees and weeps. Clint reloads.)* I don't understand. I don't understand what's going on.

CLINT. It took me a while to figure it out. Most people don't get to see what really happens. People get grabbed, people get eaten. Nobody sees a thing. But if you're patient, and quiet, and you sit and you watch...

EVAN. Jesus. I can't stop shaking. I need a drink. Jesus. *(He picks the flask up from off the ground, uncaps it, sits down in the chair and takes a long pull.)*

CLINT. At the end, when the disease takes hold... all of the memories of the victims come bubbling up to the surface. Maybe these zombies don't have thoughts and feelings of their own... maybe... maybe they eat other people to somehow capture their essence, their emotions... so they can feel something again.

EVAN. I don't... God, I don't feel good. My stomach is twisted... tied up in knots... *(From behind Evan, Clint puts the shotgun on the ground, and pulls a pair of shiny handcuffs from his pocket.)*

CLINT. I understand, son. I know exactly what you're going through. *(Evan sits down, and Clint springs into action - he grabs Evan's wrist, slaps the handcuff on it, then twists it back and grabs for Evan's other arm. Evan fights to get free.)* Hold still. Hold still, you stupid son of a bitch.

EVAN. What the - what the hell do you think you're doing?! *(Clint wrenches Evan's other arm back and locks on the other handcuff through the back of the chair. Evan continues to struggle, futilely.*

CLINT. Just sit still...

EVAN. *(Screaming.)* Help me!!! Help!!! Somebody, help me, please! Help me! Help!

CLINT. Bah, quit your yapping, you zombie-infested fuck. You think anybody cares enough to help you? There's nobody in this whole goddamn world that gives two shits about you. So shut the fuck up.

EVAN. Please, man, please. Don't do this. Don't do this. Whatever you think of me, please, don't do this. Look, I'm not one of them! I'm not! I'm a human being, just like you!

CLINT. You're a human right now. That won't last long.

EVAN. What do you mean? *(Clint picks up the flask and chugs the rest of it.)*

CLINT. You've been bit.

EVAN. What? No - no, I haven't. That's ridiculous.

CLINT. See that blood coming from your arm?

EVAN. That's... I probably caught it against the metal siding of the RV when you dragged me out...

CLINT. Nah. You remember that bald fucker with the yellow eyes who came through the window of the RV? I was watching him through binoculars, saw him take a big old juicy bite out of your arm. Last thing he did before I put a bullet in his head.

EVAN. Wait... you... you were watching me? You were watching me, and you let that thing... you let that thing bite me???

CLINT. Of course I did. I've been waiting on a moment like this for weeks now, waiting for the same zombie to grab ahold of someone. Almost got my chance at the Piggly Wiggly in Gastonia, but the lady bled out before I could get to her. I almost lost hope... and then I saw you getting out of your rust-colored Coachman in the woods... and I knew I'd found my mark. *(Evan sputters, then chokes a bit, and vomits on the floor beside him. Clint ignores him and continues talking.)* Eight minutes. First the tremors, then the nausea. Right on schedule. Anyway, in the end, it was pretty easy. All I had to do was lead the zombie pack over to your little clearing, and wait for them to do their thing. It was simple... not like you were smart enough to properly barricade your home, or put the lights out at night.

EVAN. *(Beginning to slur his words.)* You're crazy. Nobody would do that. You led them to me? You wanted them to bite me? Why? Why would you...? *(Clint crosses to the other side of the stage, finds a folding chair, and drags it over so he can sit next to Evan. He glances at his watch, then at the puddle of vomit on the floor.)*

CLINT. I'd managed to protect my family, to keep my wife and my daughter safe, since the very first hordes started invading our towns. We kept on the move. I scrounged for supplies, and my wife Marsha kept an eye on Matilda. That was my daughter's name. Matilda. Eight years old, never lost that childlike innocence, even when... even in the worst... *(Evan slumps in his seat, gurgling. Clint gets up from his seat and starts pacing back and forth as Evan gasps for air.)* I was coming back from a Chevron station in Athens when I saw the zombie mob breaking through the steel shutters on the house. I ran, and I ran, and by the time I'd gotten there... my wife was gone. My daughter was gone. That goddamn bald bastard was staring at me with those unholy yellow eyes, and I knew - I knew, if it was the last thing I'd ever do... I'd get my chance to say goodbye. *(Evan takes one last deep breath and then dies with a long sigh. Clint goes over and sits down in his chair, waiting.)* I'm sorry, kid. I'm sorry you had to go out this way. If there was... if there was only some other way... *(Evan stirs in his chair. Clint kneels in front of Evan, peering eagerly.)* Marsha? Marsha? Can you hear me? Are you in there?

EVAN. *(In Marsha's voice.)* Clint? Clint, is that you?

CLINT. *(Taking Evan's hand.)* I'm here, baby. I'm here.

EVAN. You weren't there... you were gone when--

CLINT. I know, Marsha. I know. I'm so sorry. I'm so sorry.

EVAN. It's all right. It's all right, my darling. *(He struggles against the handcuffs.)* My hands... why are they chained together...?

CLINT. Oh, my love, I'm so sorry. Here. Let me help you with that... *(Clint reaches back and unlocks the handcuffs, then moves back around in front of Evan, who puts his arms around Clint's shoulders as he weeps.)*

EVAN. Shhh, shhh, it's all right. It's all right. It's not your fault. It's not your fault. You were always there for us... *(Evan, as Marsha, begins fading. Clint reaches over and holds the hands of his wife, gazing into her face.)*

CLINT. I love you, Marsha. I always have. Ever since we were in grade school together. When we moved into that tiny apartment in Anderson. When Matilda came along. When we had that miscarriage, when we fought, and when we would make up. I've always loved you. I always will.

EVAN. I love you... I love you, too... *(He slumps over again as Marsha dies. Clint remains holding Evan's hands as, slowly, the glimmer of his child Matilda lights up Evan's face.)* Daddy?

CLINT. Oh, my Matilda. Oh, my sweet baby girl. *(He grabs Evan and hugs him tightly, sobbing as he does.)*

EVAN. I miss you, Daddy.

CLINT. I miss you, too. It's okay, baby. You don't have to be afraid. I'll be with you soon. It's okay. Daddy will be with you soon... *(Evan shudders again, slumps over, and then Matilda dies. Clint staggers back a bit, and collapses in a heap. After a pause, Evan begins reanimating, reaching out for Clint, who remains on the floor, looking up at him. Simultaneously, Karin begins crawling over from where she had fallen onto the floor, groaning and hissing.)* All right, you zombie sons of bitches. All right. Come and get me. Come and get me. You bite me, I blast your fucking head off, and then my wife and my child get one more chance to live. It's all right, you sons of bitches. It's all right. Come and get me. Come and get me. *(Karin cackles. Evan lunges at Clint and begins feasting on him. Clint screams, and as the lights go down, we hear a shot...)*

END OF PLAY

OPEN MIC NIGHT

by Evan Baughfman

Surprises await audience members at a mysterious "Open Mic" performance.

CHARACTERS

LILY
Female, 33; a performer with special talents.

MICHAEL
Male, 35; invited by Lily to sit front-and-center for the show.

MIKE
Male, 35; also invited by Lily to sit front-and-center for the show.

MAN 1
Male, any age; a supportive audience member.

MAN 2
Male, any age; a supportive audience member.

SETTING

Inside a tiny performance space with a stage. Up-center-stage, a single microphone stands.

***

Inside a tiny performance space with a stage. A few tables with chairs are organized ahead of the little stage, but only Michael, 35, is in the audience at the moment. Wearing a white polo shirt and jeans, he sits at the table closest to the microphone, front and center.

It's clear that Michael's been here for a while. He's bored. Growing antsy.

MICHAEL. *(Softly, to himself.)* The hell is taking so long…? *(He pulls a phone from a pocket, fiddles with it for a few moments. Smacks it a couple of times. He tosses the useless phone onto the table. Cups his hands around his mouth and shouts…)* HELLO? LILY? ANYONE? GONNA GET ON WITH THIS ANYTIME SOON, OR WHAT? *(No one replies. He claps his hands together in mock applause.)* GREAT SHOW, EVERYONE! BRAVO! *(He's still met with silence. He shakes his head. Sighs.)* The hell kinda joke is this? Got hidden cameras around here, or…? *(As he looks around him, another man enters the room. This is Mike, also 35, and also wearing a white polo shirt and jeans. He's holding a bouquet of flowers, though. The two men notice each other immediately. Mike stops in his tracks.)*

MIKE. Are you the only other…?

MICHAEL. Yeah, so far.

MIKE. Are you performing, or…?

MICHAEL. No. You?

MIKE. No. Thought this place would be packed. Had trouble finding it. GPS had me going in circles…

MICHAEL. Looks like there's plenty of room. Sit anywhere you like.

MIKE. Think you're at my table. My date told me to sit right up front. That it would be reserved for me.

MICHAEL. Funny. Because the person I'm here to see told me the same exact thing.

MIKE. I'm here for Lily. *(Michael leans back in his chair. Crosses his arms over his chest.)*

MICHAEL. That's interesting. I'm here for Lily, too.

MIKE. I'm going to guess she told you to dress like that?

MICHAEL. "White dress shirt and blue jeans."

MIKE. "Crisp but casual."

MICHAEL. "For our fun and special night." Yeah. Exactly what she texted me. She double-booked us.

MIKE. Have you seen her?

MICHAEL. Haven't seen anyone, but the door was open. Been here for twenty minutes, bored outta my skull.

MIKE. Is she even here? Backstage, maybe? I'm going to call her. *(He puts the flowers down on a table, takes out his phone. But his device won't work, either.)* Why won't it…? I just had it charging in the car.

MICHAEL. Same thing's going on with mine, too. *(Mike attempts to restart his phone. Unsuccessfully.)*

MIKE. Why would it just… stop working? Yours, too, since you've been here?

MICHAEL. Yep. *(Gesturing to the flowers.)* Those for her? Lily?

MIKE. Lilies for Lily.

MICHAEL. So you're that kinda guy. Likes wordplay. Puns.

MIKE. They're congratulatory flowers, for a job well done. Tradition, you know?

MICHAEL. Yeah. "...for a job well done." You ever seen her do this before? Even know what we're here to see? She a singer? A dancer? A poet? God, I hope she's not a poet…

MIKE. *(Shrugs.)* She invited me to her open mic thing, so I came. No matter how good she is or what she does, it takes guts to be up on a stage. That alone deserves recognition. That's what the flowers are for. Just trying to be thoughtful.

MICHAEL. "Thoughtful" … Yeah, alright, buddy. What you're thinking about is sucking up to her so you can get inside her pants. It looks like we've got ourselves a healthy, little competition brewing here.

MIKE. A competition for what?

MICHAEL. For Lily's affection! To see who gets to pollinate that flower first! Duh! *(Mike stares at Michael for a few seconds. Tries to process what he's just heard.)* What? You don't appreciate my wordplay?

MIKE. If you're my "competition," I think I'll do just fine.

MICHAEL. Let's do this, then!

MIKE. You really think she did this on purpose? Like, this is a game to her, or something?

MICHAEL. I don't know much about this chick or what she's into. Just saw those pics and swiped right. You know what I mean. Yeah. She told you about this, to meet out here in the middle of nowhere. What time. What to wear. And here you are.

MIKE. Here I am.

MICHAEL. And here I am. Front and center, not going anywhere. You can go, or you can have a seat at any of these other tables. Up to you, buddy. *(Mike seems hesitant at first about whether he should stay or go. But he ultimately picks up the flowers… and takes a seat at Michael's table, right across from the other guy. He puts the flowers down between the two of them.)* Seriously? Alright, buddy. This is gonna be fun. *(He extends a hand.)* I'm Michael, by the way.

MIKE. *(Shaking Michael's hand.)* Me, too. I go by Mike, though.

MICHAEL. She's got a thing for Michaels, eh? Well, may the best Michael win.

MIKE. Don't mind if I do.

MICHAEL. *(Chuckling.)* We'll see about that! *(Two other men enter: Man 1 and Man 2. They wear all black. Sit at separate tables, near the entrance.)* You guys not get the memo about the dress code? Oh, and you forgot your flowers. *(Man 1 and Man 2 look at Michael but don't say a word.)* Lemme guess… You're Michael 3, and you're Michael 4. *(Again, Man 1 and Man 2 don't speak. But they do look at each other and exchange smiles. Then, a woman, Lily, 33, wearing a stained art smock, enters the stage.)*

MIKE. There she is! *(Waving.)* Lily! Hi! *(Michael hoots and hollers. Whistles at her.)*

MICHAEL. *(To Mike.)* Not as hot as her pics, but she'll do.

LILY. *(Into the microphone.)* Good evening, everybody! Welcome! Glad you could make it to Open Mic Night! If you've never attended one of my events before, I can assure you, you're in for a real treat! Something you'll never forget! *(Man 1 and Man 2 loudly applaud. Cheer, even.)* Those guys know what I'm talking about! Let's get started, shall we?

MICHAEL. Finally!

LILY. Everyone, give a round of applause for our first performer of the evening… Michael Henderson! *(Man 1 and Man 2 applaud. Lily applauds. But Mike and Michael don't. They're confused.)*

MICHAEL. The hell…?

MIKE. Is that you? Michael Henderson?

MICHAEL. Yeah. *(To Lily.)* What is this? What're you doing?

LILY. Come on up, Michael. Don't be shy.

MICHAEL. I came to see you. I don't do… that. Perform…

LILY. Performance issues? It's okay, Michael. I can help with that. *(She closes her eyes. Lifts her hands, palms facing upward. She chants…)* Venite ad me: Michael Henderson. Et audi verba mea. Tantum verba mea. Venite ad me: Michael Henderson. Et audi verba mea. Tantum verba mea. *(The lights flicker while she speaks.)*

MICHAEL. Is that a poem? God, it is... And it's not even in English!

MIKE. What. Is. Happening?

LILY. VENITE AD ME: MICHAEL HENDERSON! ET AUDI VERBA MEA! TANTUM VERBA MEA! *(Michael suddenly stands at his seat, rigid in posture. The lights stop flickering.)* Looks like he's ready, folks! Give him another round of applause! Michael Henderson, come on up! *(Lily, Man 1, and Man 2 applaud Michael as he steps up on-stage, like he's in some kind of trance. He stands beside Lily, near the microphone.)* Michael, how are you doing tonight? Feel free to use the microphone.

MICHAEL. *(Into the microphone, robotically.)* I am a little nervous, but I am okay. I will listen to your words.

LILY. Fantastic. Glad we're on the same page. Now, Michael, you are what most people would call a "terrible human being," are you not? Answer honestly. *(As they converse, Lily and Michael pass the microphone back and forth between themselves.)*

MICHAEL. That is accurate. I am an Internet troll. I cheat on my taxes. I never recycle.

LILY. And how do you typically treat a woman, Michael? Respectfully? Or like she's a piece of trash?

MICHAEL. It depends. What has she done for me lately?

LILY. Sounds about right. A regular "pig," aren't you? Can

you squeal for us, Michael? *(Michael squeals like a pig. He really gets into it, too. On all-fours. Others applaud, even Mike, who seems to be wondering if Michael's been a part of the show all along...)* Excellent! Now, I know you came here with the intentions of making me "scream". But I think it's safe to say you'll be the one screaming tonight. Scream for us, Michael. SCREAM! *(Michael screams! A bloodcurdling shriek. Again, his "performance" gets applause.)* Impressive! We'll probably be hearing more of that later, won't we? Now, lie down, Michael. Right here, behind me. Face-up. *(Michael does just this. Lies down on the stage behind Lily, face-up.)* Good, good. Now, stay still. I'll be getting back to you soon. *(She turns her attention to Mike.)* Hello, Mike. Michael Gregory Quinn. Enjoying the show?

MIKE. It's… um… You're a hypnotist? That's cool. I've never been hypnotized before.

LILY. No, not a hypnotist. What I do is a little more… spellbinding. Magical.

MIKE. Oh. A… a magician!

LILY. Not exactly. *(Pointing.)* Are those flowers for me? What a charmer. Tell us… Is that "charm" what got you off that sexual assault charge back when you were in college?

MIKE. Hey! What are you--

LILY. Did that same "charm" help you get away with what you did to your colleague last year? Or that woman in the sports bar the summer before?

MIKE. What…? How do you…? *(He gets up from his seat, but Man 1 and Man 2 are already out of theirs. They push him back into the chair. Hold him there.)* HEY! WHAT THE HELL!

LILY. I know who you are, Mike. There's no hiding yourself from me. I have ways to learn what I need. To get what I want. I've studied for many years under the guidance of amazing women. Powerful women. Angry, talented women. Understand? Or should I spell it out for you some more? Which part needs further clarification?

MIKE. Wh... Why am I here? I... I've never--

LILY. We are ridding this world of men like you. Men like him. *(She points to Michael. He waves to her.)* STAY STILL! (Michael complies, putting his hand down.)

MIKE. What do you want from me?

LILY. I want you afraid. To feel powerless. To know that your phone won't help you because of what I did to it. You've got absolutely no place to go… nowhere to turn… because of me. I am in control. Over Michael, here. Soon, over you. So… Are you scared yet? Is it working?

MIKE. *(Looking at Man 1 and Man 2.)* Y… Yes.

LILY. A while back, I had a neighbor named Mike. He seemed like a nice enough guy. But then… one night, I woke up, and there he was… in my bedroom… with a knife in his hand. He told me to be quiet, not to make a peep. But he didn't know who I was… what I could do… not until I made him stab himself again and again and again, right in his rotten excuse for a heart. I'm an artist… painter, mostly… At the time, I was having trouble with my work… coming up with something new… original… Seeing his blood, all over my clean sheets… it inspired me. *(She removes a long, sharp knife from her smock.)*

MIKE. OH, GOD, NO!

LILY. Don't look away! I'd really like an audience for this! *(Man 1 and Man 2 hold Mike down more firmly than before, forcing him to look forward.)* Can't stand that name anymore. Mike. Makes me sick. I find monsters named Michael… quite a few of you around, actually… and I do these open mic events as my way to make the world a safer place for all… Get it yet? This is not an "Open Mic Night," like you probably thought. *(She taps the microphone.*

Shakes her head. Aims the knife's point in Mike's direction.) No. It's an "Open Mike Night"… as in I'm going to open. You. Up. With. This.

MICHAEL. I get it now. That is some really clever wordplay.

LILY. SHUT UP!

MIKE. *(Struggling under Man 1 and Man 2.)* PLEASE, DON'T DO THIS! PLEASE!

LILY. Hmmm… What did you do when those women said that same exact thing to you? *(She stands over Michael. Gazes at the knife.)* What I do is art. Just not something you could really appreciate. But it sells. Hangs in galleries around the world. Inside museums with eclectic tastes. I'm huge in Eastern Europe. You see, the white shirt's like a blank canvas. Spurting blood is an expressive but unpredictable medium. No two canvases are ever truly alike. *(She looks to Mike.)* Your performance… what you produce for me up here on this stage… will be its own unique piece of work.

MIKE. MICHAEL! MICHAEL, YOU'VE GOT TO FIGHT HER, MAN! FIGHT BACK! *(Man 1 smacks Mike across the face. Man 2 punches him in the gut. Mike slouches over. Groans.)*

LILY. *(To Man 1 and Man 2.)* Be a little gentler with him, okay? We've got to keep his kidneys in good condition if we're going to get full market value for them!

MIKE. YOU'RE INSANE!

LILY. No matter what I do, I will always be a better person than scumbags like you! *(She turns to Michael.)* Michael, sit up for me, now. Face our audience. *(Michael sits up straight. Faces the audience.)* Was going to do this myself, but I think this will terrify Mike even more. Take the knife, Michael. *(Michael takes the knife from Lily. Studies it.)*

MIKE. OH, GOD! STAB HER, MICHAEL! GO ON! GET

HER RIGHT IN THE-- *(Man 1 and Man 2 rough up Mike some more, leaving him gasping for breath.)*

LILY. No, no, no. You do as I say. Don't you, Michael?

MICHAEL. Whatever you say, Lily.

LILY. Then, use the knife on yourself, Michael. Don't be shy. Be open. Go ahead! Punish yourself! Scream! NOW, MICHAEL! LET'S MAKE SOME ART! *(Mike protests. And right as Michael plunges the knife into own chest… cut to black.)*

END OF PLAY

SACRIFICE

By Jacquelyn Priskorn

What does "sacrifice" truly mean? You'd better be sure you know when making a sacrifice to The Great Deity.

CHARACTERS

SACRIFICE
A woman, bound and gagged, about to be "sacrificed".

LEADER
The leader of this mysterious sect.

ACOLYTE 1
An acolyte of this mysterious sect.

ACOLYTE 2
An acolyte of this mysterious sect.

**Various other acolytes as desired.*

SETTING

A place where one might have a sacrifice.

SACRIFICE by Jacquelyn Priskorn

***

Demonic chanting is heard. A woman, tied and gagged, is dragged on stage by cloaked acolytes who continue to chant over her muffled cries.

ACOLYTES. Kan duh huna Kan duh chu kan duh a ni.

LEADER. Oh, Great Deity, we bring to you this sacrifice.

ACOLYTES. Kan duh huna Kan duh chu kan duh a ni.

LEADER. We ask that you accept this life, this blood, this flesh. We ask that you give us your favor so that we may bring glory to your name.

ACOLYTES. Kan duh huna Kan duh chu kan duh a ni.

LEADER. We give so much glory to your name, but we want to know you hear us. So we give you this sacrifice.

ACOLYTES. I tan thah kan duh a ni.

LEADER. We will now allow the sacrifice to speak, so you can hear her fear of your great power. So that her fear may feed you, please you and move you to reward us for this sacrifice to you. Let the sacrifice be heard! *(The gag is removed from her as she squirms. She opens her mouth wide as if to scream, but then she just adjusts her jaw and sticks out her tongue in reaction to a bad taste.)*

SACRIFICE. Ugh. That tasted terrible. *(The Leader seems a little thrown off by this, but shakes it off, continuing the ceremony.)*

LEADER. Hear her cry and accept this sacrifice--

SACRIFICE. Hold up. How exactly is killing ME a sacrifice for YOU?

LEADER. What?

SACRIFICE. Isn't the definition of sacrifice "To give up something precious?" Am I precious to any of you? *(Awkward silence.)* Do any of you even know my name? *(More awkward silence.)* So, really, none of you would suffer if I were to die? That isn't a real sacrifice.

ACOLYTE 1. Well, I do have to clean up after. That's not easy.

ACOLYTE 2. Oh, that's true! It gets messy here. Jerry can be here scrubbing for hours.

SACRIFICE. Do you think that's enough suffering to be considered a sacrifice?

ACOLYTE 1. It's pretty gross.

SACRIFICE. Not going to take that personally.

ACOLYTE 2. You shouldn't. It's just business.

LEADER. Do not converse with the sacrifice!

SACRIFICE. Ah! But that's what we're debating here, right? Whether or not killing me is actually a sacrifice or not.

LEADER. It is!

ACOLYTE 2. Ah ah ah! Don't converse with the sacrifice!

LEADER. The Great Deity demands flesh and blood to prove our devotion.

SACRIFICE. Well, that's different than a sacrifice, isn't it? I mean, you could pick a scab and lay it on your altar. Flesh and blood. Bam.

ACOLYTE 1. Our deity is more of an "all or nothing" deity.

SACRIFICE. I see.

LEADER. She shouldn't see! Who forgot the blindfold?

ACOLYTE 2. I dropped it in a puddle.

LEADER. So?

ACOLYTE 2. I don't know what kind of puddle! It was gross!

LEADER. This is a sacrifice!

ACOLYTE 1. It was gross, though.

LEADER. Sack-Ree-Fice!

SACRIFICE. Yeah, you need to risk a little leptospirosis to make your deity happy, kids.

LEADER. That's not what I'm saying.

SACRIFICE. But you get what I'm saying, right? Murdering a random stranger is hardly a sacrifice.

ACOLYTE 1. Well, I mean, we could get arrested for murder if someone caught us.

ACOLYTE 2. Oh yeah. Jail would suck.

LEADER. But you WON'T get arrested. You're all on the police force or work in the D.A's office. We've talked about this.

ACOLYTE 1. Still, the risk is there.

SACRIFICE. But not really. What could you lose? What would you truly miss if you killed me?

ACOLYTE 2. I rather enjoyed stalking you the last few days.

ACOLYTE 1. Right!? You go to such interesting places!

ACOLYTE 2. I never even knew we had an art museum in town.

SACRIFICE. But the art museum will still be there, even if I'm not.

ACOLYTE 2. True.

ACOLYTE 1. But I enjoyed watching you enjoy that art. I'll miss those times.

ACOLYTE 2. You were a true connoisseur.

SACRIFICE. Still not a sacrifice.

ACOLYTE 2. No?

SACRIFICE. You'll move on to your next sacrifice to stalk eventually. You won't have a gaping hole in your life where I used to be.

ACOLYTE 2. Just a gaping hole where your heart used to be.

SACRIFICE. Really?

ACOLYTE 1. That's where all the blood is.

LEADER. This needs to stop.

ACOLYTE 2. You're right, dear Leader. This sacrifice has removed the leptospirosis blindfold from all of our eyes.

LEADER. The what?

ACOLYTE 1. I get it now. This is just a party where we kill a stranger at the end.

ACOLYTE 2. A party where we have to clean up after!

ACOLYTE 1. And provide our own cleaning supplies!

LEADER. You really don't want to--

ACOLYTE 1. Look, you're an extremely charismatic leader. It's hard to tell you "No." But, here it goes... No.

LEADER. No?

ACOLYTE 2. We can't just blindly murder for you or The Great Deity anymore. We have questions. We admit, we probably should have asked them before the first five sacrifices...

ACOLYTE 1. Hindsight's 20/20.

ACOLYTE 2. For sure. But, we're asking questions now.

ACOLYTE 1. And we're letting you go.

SACRIFICE. Really?

LEADER. Don't!

ACOLYTE 1. You're right. Killing you isn't a sacrifice. We should only do what would truly please The Great Deity. This isn't truth.

ACOLYTE 2. A murder masquerading as a sacrifice is really just a blasphemous lie, isn't it? *(The acolytes release the sacrifice.)*

SACRIFICE. You're right. *(The sacrifice stretches with her newfound freedom.)* The Great Deity loves the truth. Another thing you're right about? All the blood is in the heart.

ACOLYTE 1. I knew it! Wait, what? *(The Sacrifice makes a powerful gesture, plunging the room into darkness with the sound of a vault door slamming shut. There is chaos. Screams, people trying to get out. An otherworldly screech. The sound of flesh ripping and squelching. Bones snapping. A large mouth slurps and chews as people fight for their lives, they are being eaten alive. Bodies hit the floor until the only sound is a slurping, chewing mouth of enormous size. The lights come back up to reveal The Sacrifice standing over the bodies of Acolyte 1 and Acolyte 2, their hearts in each of her hands held high above her own head. She squeezes the last of the crimson juice into her mouth. The Leader stands by in silent shock. Satisfied, The Sacrifice drops the hearts to the ground with a splat. She shivers in ecstasy.)*

SACRIFICE. The truth is delicious!

LEADER. You ate them all.

SACRIFICE. Okay! Well, I guess I'll find you when you have your next sect assembled.

LEADER. Who's going to clean this up?

SACRIFICE. Thank you for your sacrifice. *(She releases a wet and monstrous belch.)*

END OF PLAY

THE DEAL

by Ryan Kaminski

A short horror/thriller play set in the mid-1950s. A widow is visited by a sinister stranger looking to collect one of her husband's unique outstanding debts.

CHARACTERS

VIVIAN HOWARD
Female, 30s-40s. High maintenance, proper etiquette, sickeningly sweet.

ARTHUR NELLIGAN
Male, 40s-50s. Articulate, refined, dapper, sophisticated.

SETTING

The front porch of Vivian Howard's home. Louisiana.

Sometime in the mid-1950's.

THE DEAL by Ryan Kaminski

***

Three steps lead to a sweeping front porch. The porch consists of a small table beside a chair and a second chair near the front door. Vivian Howard sits in the chair beside the table. She wears a white dress and a crucifix around her neck. One of her fingers has been heavily bandaged. A pitcher of lemonade, a glass, and a radio rest on the table beside a check. Vivian picks up the check and examines it while fiddling with the radio. A Jazz song plays. She laughs.

VIVIAN. *(To herself.)* My, my, my… *(Pours herself a glass of lemonade and toasts the glass to the radio.)* Here's to you, Billy Boy… *(She sets down the glass along with the check and rises. She starts dancing and twirling to the beat of a trumpet solo. She dances in the porch corner, lost in her own little world. Arthur Nelligan enters Stage Left. He wears a burgundy suit and a black tie. He carries a case. He climbs up the porch steps where Vivian continues to dance. The radio reception flickers at his arrival, causing Vivian to turn around and notice him. She becomes startled.)*

ARTHUR. I'm sorry, I didn't mean to frighten you! *(Vivian rushes over to the radio and flicks it off.)*

VIVIAN. No, no, the fault is mine. I'm afraid, I forgot my manners. Here I am taking a dance break like a silly little girl when I have a visitor… *(Notices his suit.)* …a very distinguished visitor.

ARTHUR. *(Gestures to the radio.)* Was that William Howard on the trumpet, by any chance?

VIVIAN. Yes. Yes, it was.

ARTHUR. Thought so. I never fail to recognize a signature Howard solo. Nobody could play the trumpet quite like Billy Boy. My name is Arthur Nelligan. *(Shakes her hand.)*

And you must be Vivian, a.k.a "Billy Boy's" wife?

VIVIAN. I am. I mean, I was. I mean, I'm not sure if you heard but…

ARTHUR. I'm sorry, I didn't mean to word it like that. Yes, I know all about the accident. Saw it on the news and I passed by the bridge on the way over. Forgive me, this was not the way I meant to introduce myself…

VIVIAN. How's about we start over then?

ARTHUR. Fine by me.

VIVIAN. What exactly can I do for you this evening, Mr. Nelligan?

ARTHUR. Believe it or not, but I'm here to bring you something. Something that belonged to your late husband.

VIVIAN. Bring me something? Are you saying you knew William?

ARTHUR. I did. Met him in New Orleans when he was a starving artist working at a voodoo shop in the French Quarter.

VIVIAN. Goodness! That must've been ages ago!

ARTHUR. It was. It was right before he caught his big break at the Jackson Club.

VIVIAN. Oh, the Jackson! It's been years since I was there. William and I would go all the time. They hung his picture on the wall and everything.

ARTHUR. I was in the audience the night he first played there. He was just a scared, scrawny kid back then, willing to do whatever it took to prove himself. The audience certainly wasn't on his side when they first laid eyes on him. That was until he started to play. The rest is history.

VIVIAN. That's really amazing you were there when it happened.

ARTHUR. It was quite the night to say the least. A much cooler night for certain… *(Pulls out a handkerchief from his breast pocket and tabs at his forehead.)*

VIVIAN. Goodness, you must be hot. Especially in a suit like that. How's about some lemonade to cool you off?

ARTHUR. Sounds lovely.

VIVIAN. Great. Have a seat and I'll be back with another glass. *(She pulls over the second chair and places it at the table. She then exits through the front door. Arthur sits and notices the check. He picks it up and examines it. Vivian reenters with a second glass. She notices him holding the check.)*

ARTHUR. Goodness… *(Drops the check.)* Now I'm the one who's forgotten their manners. I'm sorry, I didn't mean to pry. I was looking at it because I wasn't sure what it was.

VIVIAN. It's quite all right. *(Pours him a glass.)* Life insurance people brought it earlier this afternoon. Never even realized he had life insurance. I've always been a bit of a scatterbrain with money, especially when it's unexpected money. I guess I haven't gotten a chance to bring it inside yet. *(Her crucifix dangles in front of Arthur as she pours. He quickly looks away from it, but not before noticing her arm. He then scoops up his glass and drinks.)*

ARTHUR. Whoa…

VIVIAN. Something wrong?

ARTHUR. No. I just didn't expect it to be so sweet.

VIVIAN. Want to know a secret? *(Pause.)* All my friends think it's homemade, but I just use frozen lemonade and pour in some extra sugar.

ARTHUR. Interesting. Well, like I always say: "we all have our secrets." *(Gestures to her arm.)* What happened there? Those aren't burn marks, are they?

VIVIAN. *(Takes an extra-long sip of lemonade.)* I'm afraid I was rather careless with the stove a while back. I can be quite the klutz at times as you can see… *(Gestures to her bandaged finger.)* You said you had something for me?

ARTHUR. Yes. Keep in mind, I've tried to keep this in decent condition over the years. *(He sets the case on the table and opens it. He pulls out a trumpet and hands it to her.)*

VIVIAN. Oh my…

ARTHUR. One of William's first trumpets. In fact, it was the first trumpet he played as "Billy Boy" Howard.

VIVIAN. Wait… *(Examines it.)* Are you telling me this is the trumpet he played that night at the Jackson?

ARTHUR. That it is. Look here if you don't believe me. *(He pulls out a pamphlet from the case. Vivien reads it over.)*

VIVIAN. My goodness. This is a pamphlet from the club that night. It's dated and everything! I do declare… *(Gestures to the trumpet.)* How on earth did you get this?

ARTHUR. It was my mine originally. You see, the night before William was set to play at the Jackson, he dropped his only trumpet off the fire escape at his apartment. He desperately needed a new trumpet, so I let him borrow mine.

VIVIAN; That was very kind of you. If you don't mind me asking, why did you hang onto the pamphlet for all these years?

ARTHUR. Because I knew William would be heading straight for the top after that performance. I knew the items from that night would be worth something someday.

VIVIAN. You were right there. I know many of William's fans who would pay top dollar for these things. Especially now… *(Pause.)* I just can't believe you came all the way out here to give them to me.

ARTHUR. Now that you mention it, there is another reason for my presence this evening…

VIVIAN. Oh?

ARTHUR. You see, I'm afraid your husband owed me something. Something he failed to deliver.

VIVIAN. I see. Well, Mr. Nelligan, it embarrasses me to say this, but you're not the first person whom William was indebted to. Tell you what: how about in the morning, we go to my lawyer and see if we can work something out?

ARTHUR. I'm afraid your lawyer would be useless in this case.

VIVIAN. I don't understand.

ARTHUR. Flip the pamphlet over and read… *(Vivian turns the pamphlet over and reads a hand-written inscription at the top.)*

VIVIAN. "I, William Howard, do solemnly swear, that in exchange for my success, my fame, and my fortune, I will grant Mr. Arthur Nelligan…"

ARTHUR. *(Sips his lemonade.)* Finish it…

VIVIAN. "…complete and total ownership over my soul…"

ARTHUR. You'll see the initials are written in blood as is the date.

VIVIAN. What on earth is this?

ARTHUR. It's a contract, Mrs. Howard, signed and dated by your husband. It states that in exchange for me giving him the fame and fortune he so desired in life, I was to receive ownership over his soul at the time of his death.

VIVIAN. I'm not sure what kind of game you're playing, but it's not funny…

ARTHUR. I agree, there's nothing funny about it. Just like there's nothing funny about those cigarette burns on your arms. *(Pause.)* Come on Mrs. Howard, we both know you didn't burn yourself on the stove. Billy Boy used to put his cigarettes out on you when he got drunk. He told me himself.

VIVIAN. And when did he tell you this?

ARTHUR. About an hour or two after he died.

VIVIAN. Okay, I'm calling the police... *(Attempts to rise.)*

ARTHUR. Go ahead. The police have no power over me. No man does...

VIVIAN. STOP IT! Stop it right now and tell me who you really are!

ARTHUR. Who I really am? Over the years, I've gone by many names, for I was present when the earth began. I've soared above your skies as an angel, slithered through your gardens as a snake, and walked among your people as a charming stranger. Through it all, man has looked to me for guidance, and often turned to me as a last resort. I am whatever man needs me to, and in the case of your husband, I was the one who could make all his dreams come true. And as part of the deal we made, I was promised a soul; a soul which I have yet to collect. *(He stares at her intently. Vivian stares into his eyes and shudders.)*

VIVIAN. Oh my God...

ARTHUR. You can see it in my eyes now, can't you? You can see that I'm telling you the truth.

VIVIAN. If my husband promised you his soul, then what are you doing here? My husband is dead, so why don't you have his soul yet?

ARTHUR. Because the man who promised me his soul wasn't the same man who drove off that bridge. The man who promised me his soul, still had a soul worth collecting. But over the years, he let his fame and fortune destroy everything that made his soul pure. He cheated, he lied, he stole, and most of all, he delighted in abusing you. Such crimes made his soul rot, and I cannot take a rotten soul.

VIVIAN. Then what do you want from me?

ARTHUR. Isn't it obvious? When your husband died, you

inherited all his fortune, which means, you also inherited all his debts…

VIVIAN. No. No, you can't be serious…!

ARTHUR. You know I am, or else I wouldn't be here. As part of my deal, I need a soul that's fresh and pure, and with Billy Boy's soul as black as night, I'm afraid, I'm left with yours.

VIVIAN. No. Please! No, my soul is far from pure…

ARTHUR. It's pure compared to your husband's. The man committed every crime short of murder. And because of that I need…

VIVIAN. What did you just say?

ARTHUR. What?

VIVIAN. About my husband's crimes?

ARTHUR. I said he committed every crime short of murder.

VIVIAN. And does murder blacken the soul?

ARTHUR. Of course, it does. Does a God-fearing woman like yourself really need to ask me that? *(Vivian starts to laugh. She laughs and laughs until Arthur becomes annoyed.)* Why're you laughing? Is this somehow funny to you?

VIVIAN. No. What's funny is you never asked me about my finger.

ARTHUR. Your finger? What're you talking about?

VIVIAN. While William did abuse me, what happened to my finger was my own doing. *(Pulls off the bandage and lets him see.)* I cut it myself. I cut it while I was puncturing the break line to his car.

ARTHUR. You… you did what…?

VIVIAN. I punctured his break line. Which means, William drove off that bridge because of me. I murdered him and I would gladly do so again. So, if murder blackens the soul, then I'm afraid my soul is as black as your tie, Mr. Nelligan.

ARTHUR. No. No! YOU'RE LYING! YOU'RE LYING… *(Vivian stares at him intently. Arthur stares into her eyes and shudders.)*

VIVIAN. You can see it in my eyes now, can't you? You can see that I'm telling you the truth. *(Arthur rips up the pamphlet in a rage.)*

ARTHUR. HOW DARE YOU! HOW DARE YOU CHEAT ME…!

VIVIAN. As you said before: we all have our secrets, don't we? *(Arthur descends the steps, and storms off Stage Left. Vivian pours herself another glass of lemonade and turns on the radio. The radio plays another Jazz song.)*

VIVIAN. *(To herself.)* My, my, my… *(Toasts the glass to the radio.)* Here's to you, Billy Boy…

END OF PLAY

THE QUAKE

by Travis Williams

After a massive earthquake rocks their quiet mountain town, best friends, Jackie and Briggs, are about to find out what has been slaughtering several woodland creatures.

CHARACTERS

JACKIE
Young girl.

BRIGGS
Young boy.

SETTING

The dark woods of a mountain town.
Now.

NOTES

The special effects within the script can be as bare or as elaborate as desired.

THE QUAKE by Travis Williams

***

Jackie is sawing off a dead deer's head.

BRIGGS. You got this, Jackie.

JACKIE. *(Struggling.)* God! Damn it! *(She stops.)*

BRIGGS. You okay?

JACKIE. I can't do this, Briggs.

BRIGGS. Course you can. You just gotta cut a little harder is all.

JACKIE. It's not as easy as it looks.

BRIGGS. You ain't never done this before?

JACKIE. You have?

BRIGGS. Couple times... you'll know when you've reached its soft spot cause it'll crack a little.

JACKIE. Gross... *(Beat.)* Screw this. *(She throws the saw down.)*

BRIGGS. What're you doin'?

JACKIE. It ain't worth it.

BRIGGS. What're you talkin' about?! We trekked all the way down the mountain to get the damn saw, then trekked all the way back--

JACKIE. --I'm sorry, okay?! I'll steal some of my Dad's cigarettes for you!

BRIGGS. Give me the damn saw. *(He picks up the saw and starts cutting.)*

JACKIE. Briggs, it don't matter any how...

BRIGGS. No... don't say that. I know it matters to ya, cause we wouldn't be up here if it didn't.

JACKIE. I don't even know what I'm expectin' him to say anyway.

BRIGGS. Probably won't believe his eyes for one.

JACKIE. For real though, what the hell am I supposed to do? Walk it up to the front door and say, 'Hey, Pa! Look! I killed it! I killed a deer! See?! I'm not a worthless piece of shit after all!' *(He stops sawing.)*

BRIGGS. You're not a piece of shit.

JACKIE. Worthless piece of shit.

BRIGGS. You ain't that neither.

JACKIE. …thanks.

BRIGGS. *(Brief pause.)* But you might wanna tell him you wanna mount it on the wall though. Otherwise he might think you're bat shit crazy bringin' a deer head home like this.

JACKIE. Probably right… *(Briggs begins sawing again. Eventually the bone snaps a little.)* Holy shit, Briggs, you got it!

BRIGGS. Told ya, just gotta keep workin' it like a termite.

JACKIE. Gross again.

BRIGGS. *(Offers Jackie the saw.)* Here.

JACKIE. What?

BRIGGS. Finish it, Jackie.

JACKIE. But I…

BRIGGS. Go on. You gotta have truth in your eyes when you show 'em. Otherwise the old man's gonna see that you're lying bout cuttin' it's head off. *(Jackie takes the saw.)* One hard quick cut oughta do it. *(She cuts the rest of the bone til is snaps and the deer head falls off.)*

JACKIE. Holy shit!

BRIGGS. See?! I told ya! *(They laugh until their laughter slowly dies down.)*

JACKIE. *(Pause.)* So… how'd you think it died?

BRIGGS. *(Clears his throat.)* Huh? Oh… I uh… I don't know. Daddy said there's been lots of dead things turnin' up lately.

JACKIE. Like dead deer?

BRIGGS. Like dead everythin', Jackie. Racoons, possums …shit, I even heard they found a dead bear behind Dale's Donut Shop. All its blood sucked dry and its insides ripped to shreds like this poor little bastard. Daddy said that quake was like a bad omen from the bible.

JACKIE. That was really scary. I saw on the news that Mount Jefferson was split wide open cause of it. Heard Pa say they're sendin' like scientist in to research it… goin' down in that cave and what not. Can you imagine what's in that thing?

BRIGGS. Could be what's doin' all this killin'.

JACKIE. Shut up.

BRIGGS. I'm serious. Daddy heard Deputy Wilks say he saw a swarm of somethin' shoot across the road the other night.

JACKIE. You're screwin' with me.

BRIGGS. Honest to God, Jackie!

JACKIE. Like what… like bats?

BRIGGS. Nah… crawlin'… like centipedes or somethin'. But like… big as cats he said.

JACKIE. Bullshit. My Pa said Deputy Wilks is a pill popper.

BRIGGS. Pill popper or not, Daddy said he was shaken up pretty bad.

JACKIE. *(Pause.)* You think he'll know I didn't kill it? Think he'll see I'm lyin'?

BRIGGS. *(Pause.)* Honestly, Jackie? I think our Daddies are too drunk to care bout the truth. Long as he's got something to spout off about at the bar he'll be happy enough.

JACKIE. "Your boy might have a mean tackle… but my

girl killed a deer with her bare hands!!"

BRIGGS. "Prove it!"

JACKIE. Then he'll toss the head up on the bar. *(They laugh.)*

BRIGGS. I can just see Earl's face, standin' there all stupefied behind the bar! His glass eye poppin' right out of his head!

JACKIE. Right into Stella Vegas' wine glass she brings from home!

BRIGGS. Oh Sweet Jesus. Her hair will grow another mile high off her head!

JACKIE. An turn another shade of purple! *(They laugh harder. Then, a sound of leaves scattering is heard.)*

BRIGGS. Shh!

JACKIE. *(Brief pause.)* You hear that too? *(A sound of a strange cricket mixed with a hiss.)* We should go …

BRIGGS. Let's get the head in the bag. *(They pick the deer head up and toss it into a duffel bag and zip it up.)*

JACKIE. Got it… you grab that end. Got it?

BRIGGS. Yeah.

JACKIE. And… lift! *(They lift the bag and begin to walk home. After a few steps…)* You can tell your Daddy too…

BRIGGS. Bout what?

JACKIE. That you helped me kill it.

BRIGGS. Nah… it's your find.

JACKIE. But then maybe he wouldn't yell at ya for drawin' and readin' comic books all the time… *(They stop walking.)* …I'm sorry.

BRIGGS. S'okay … I just didn't know you could hear all that.

JACKIE. Are trailers aren't that far apart.

BRIGGS. Yeah… *(They start walking again.)*

JACKIE. You're a really good drawer, Briggs.

BRIGGS. Thanks, Jackie.

JACKIE. I still got that picture you made… pinned on my wall.

BRIGGS. The one of us up in the hot air balloon?

JACKIE. Yeah… with me ridin' on top reachin' for the sun.

BRIGGS. That's who you are, Jackie… always reachin' and dreamin' for stuff… goin' places I'd never even think of.

JACKIE. I don't know about that… but you keep drawin' the way you do, you'll be travelin' all over cause of it. Be famous.

BRIGGS. Shit… *(They stop walking.)*

JACKIE. I'm serious. That's your ticket outta here, Briggs. While I'm stuck sawin' off deer heads to show people I'm braver than they think I am.

BRIGGS. You don't need to impress anyone, Jackie. You're plenty brave… you got lots of stuff to offer. You're real good at stories… maybe you can start writin' 'em down?

JACKIE. And what… you draw 'em up?

BRIGGS. Ain't that crazy of an idea.

JACKIE. Not too crazy at all, I guess. You're my best friend, Briggs.

BRIGGS. You're mine too, Jackie.

JACKIE. *(Pause.)* It's so quiet up here.

BRIGGS. Yeah… really is…

JACKIE. Can't even hear any birds…

BRIGGS. Yeah… ain't that somethin'… *(Silence.)* Jackie… I've been meanin' to tell you that I really--

JACKIE. Shit!

BRIGGS. Wha--What?!

JACKIE. I forgot my dad's saw!

BRIGGS. Jesus…

JACKIE. Just hold that thought, I'll be right back.

BRIGGS. No, you stay with your trophy. I'll go get it. *(He heads back to the dead deer to get the saw. To himself...)* Jackie... I've been meaning to tell you that I think you're really great and I think that together... *(Beat. Sigh.)* Forget it, Briggs... You already know she's not... *(He stops at the deer.)* The hell?

JACKIE. *(From a distance.)* Briggs, you find it?

BRIGGS. Yeah! But...

JACKIE. *(From a distance.)* But what?!

BRIGGS. *(To himself.)* It's all bent to shit... *(The sound of a strange cricket mixed with a hiss.)* Whoa... What the holy fuck are you?

JACKIE. *(From a distance.)* Briggs, let's go! It's gettin' dark!

BRIGGS. *(Calling to Jackie.)* I think I found one of those centipede things! It's all cut up! *(Jackie runs over to Briggs.)*

JACKIE. What'd you say?

BRIGGS. Look. See? Right there under the brush...

JACKIE. I can barely... Jesus look at its legs. You can see its veins pumpin' an everythin'.

BRIGGS. I know... Ugly son of a bitch ain't it? S'like Deputy Wilks said... it's as big as a cat. *(Kissing sounds.)* Here little guy... Come here. *(He moves closer to the brush.)*

JACKIE. What the hell are you doin'?

BRIGGS. Gonna kill it... bring it back with us. *(More kissing sounds.)* Come on ugly bug... Come here.

JACKIE. Briggs, seriously, I wouldn't touch that thing.

BRIGGS. It's not gonna do anything. Looks like it got hurt bendin' up your Daddy's saw. See?

JACKIE. Holy shit...

BRIGGS. Look at those veins... all purple and white... Ew! Look at its eyes. It's got green and black all swirlin' together. Creepy... *(Kissing sounds.)* Come here buggy bug bug.

JACKIE. Briggs, it's lookin' right at you. *(The sound of a strange cricket mixed with a hiss grows.)*

BRIGGS. That's it. Come'ere... Almost--

JACKIE. Briggs! *(Sound of leaves scatter.)*

BRIGGS. Jesus! *(Silence.)* Where'd it go?

JACKIE. I don't know... it... I don't know.

BRIGGS. You see how fast that damn thing-- *(Sound of leaves scatter all around. Briggs chases the sound offstage.)* Over there... You see it? I think it's-- *(From offstage a wailing screech comes from Briggs. He RE-ENTERS with the centipede stabbing its legs into his flesh. The puppet centipede should be able to move its neck and jaw to speak along with Briggs. It should appear as though the puppet is controlling Briggs so that they are one.)*

JACKIE. BRIGGS!

BRIGGS. AAAHHH!! It's diggin' it's legs into my back! IT'S DIGGIN' IT'S LEGS INTO MY BACK!!

JACKIE. What--What should I do?! What should I do?!

BRIGGS. THE SAW! USE THE SAW! CUT IT OFF! AH! GOD! CUT IT OFF OF ME!

JACKIE. Okay-- Okay! I got it. Kneel down! Come here! Kneel down! Okay. Okay. I'm gonna cut it, okay? I'm gonna cut-- *(She saws into the centipede and its shell snaps and breaks.)*

BRIGGS. *(Screams.)* NO!!! STOP! I can feel... I can feel you cutting it!

JACKIE. What?! Shit! Shit! I'm sorry! Briggs, I'm sorry!

BRIGGS. *(Woozy.)* I can feel... everything.

JACKIE. What do I do?! Briggs, What do you want me to do?!

BRIGGS. *(Very woozy.)* Don't... Don't... cut it anymore... Don't cut it.

CENTIPEDE. *(Hissing.)* Don't... Don't... cut it anymore... Don't cut it.

JACKIE. Holy fuck Briggs it's talking... That thing is talking! *(Slow slurping sound is heard from the centipede.)* Oh God... Briggs... Is that your blood going through its legs?!

BRIGGS. *(Said together with Centipede. Very woozy.)* I feel... Oh shit... I feel dizzy... I feel nnnnuuummmbbb--

CENTIPEDE. *(Said together with Briggs. Hissing.)* I feel... Oh shit... I feel dizzy... I feel nnnnuuummmbbb--

JACKIE. Briggs? Briggs! Stay with me! *(Briggs collapses to the ground.)*

BRIGGS. *(Said together with Centipede. About to pass out.)* It's... I can feel it's hhuunnggrryy...

CENTIPEDE. *(Said together with Briggs. Hissing.)* It's... I can feel it's hhuunnggrryy...

JACKIE. Briggs! Briggs look at me, please!

BRIGGS. It wants... to go in... my... my... *(The centipede pries open his mouth and moves down his throat. Briggs is choking and gagging as gruesome tearing and snapping sounds are heard.)*

JACKIE. *(Through tears.)* Briggs... I'm gonna go get help... Okay? You stay right here... I'm gonna go get-- *(Briggs convulses, moaning and grabbing his stomach as the centipede moves around inside him.)*

BRIGGS. *(Through a dislocated jaw.)* Jackie... I love-- *(The centipede bursts from his stomach. Guts and gore splatter onto the ground. Jackie vomits. The centipede begins snacking on Briggs' body.)*

JACKIE. You... SON OF A BITCH!! *(She saws at the centipede. It snaps and squirts blood. It squeals and wiggles. Out of breath...)* I got it, Briggs... I got it... I killed it... *(Begins to cry.)* I killed it... I killed it... *(The sound of leaves rustle around her as she's surrounded by more centipedes.)* There's more of you? *(The sound of a strange cricket mixed with a hiss begins again. Leaves rustle as they close in.)* Come on then... you ugly sons of bitches... Come and get me... COME AND GET ME!! *(The centipedes close in. A crescendo of screeching mixed with Jackie's screams as the lights fade.)*

END OF PLAY

UNBURIED

by John Bavoso

On a dark and stormy Halloween night (omg, so cliché, right?!?), two characters - victims of the "bury your gays" trope - both have come to life and are out for bloody revenge on their author/father. But the unexpected arrival of a fourth character leads to events none of them could have predicted.

CHARACTERS

CARTER
He/him, white, 40+. Definitely the type to wear a corduroy jacket with elbow patches or a cable knit cardigan with holes in it (or both) and glasses. Mild-mannered until he's not.

JACK
He/him, any race, in his 20s or 30s. Darkly fabulous.

LEXA
She/her, any race, in her 20s or 30s. Wiley and menacing.

OSCAR
He/him, any race, 40s+. Surprising.

SETTING

Evening, October 31. A famous novelist's study in the basement of an old house. There's a desk and swivel chair and a small couch.

***

At rise, Carter is alone in his study, talking on his phone. A storm rages outside and we can hear the thunder. Perhaps the lights flicker slightly as he talks.

CARTER. Sweetheart? Hi. While you're out, do you think you could drop by the liquor store? I'm running low on single-malt. Yes, I see it's raining, but you're already out, are you not? What's the worst that can happen... you get wetter? Perfect. No, I turned the porch light out. Not interested in distractions tonight. Get home safe. Love you, bye. *(He hangs up and takes a seat behind his desk. After a deep exhale, he cracks his knuckles and begins to type on his computer—or, even better, a typewriter. After a few moments, there's another clap of thunder and the lights go out.)* Hello? Sweetheart? *(He waits for a reply, but receiving none, moves to the fuse box.)* Seriously, a power outage during a stormy Halloween night? *(Looking upward.)* You may be omniscient, but you're a real hack writer! *(Suddenly, the lights snap back on, but it's different this time; the lighting is wrong, dim and lurid. In the blackout, Jack and Lexa have appeared, draped casually over the couch and sitting at his desk. He's gaunt, pale, in a hospital gown; she's wearing ripped clothing and has blood trickling down her forehead. Carter jumps.)* Who the hell are you?!

JACK. We'll get to that in due time, Carter.

LEXA. Why don't you take a seat? *(She stands up from the desk chair and gestures to it.)*

CARTER. How... how did you get in here?

JACK. It wasn't hard.

LEXA. We know every inch of this place - we were born here, after all.

CARTER. That's not... we've owned this house for--

JACK. Today is a day for the impossible.

LEXA. For the tables to turn. *(She spins the chair.)*

CARTER. Look, my wallet's upstairs, let me run and grab it for you...

LEXA. Ha! What would we do with money?!

JACK. Besides, we know better than to come to a writer for cash, even one as successful as you. We're dead, not brain dead.

CARTER. Did you just say you're...

JACK. Just a bit of foreshadowing. You're familiar with the concept?

CARTER. I don't know who you people are, but--

LEXA. Oh, you know us.

JACK. Better than anyone in the world.

CARTER. I really think you have me confused with someone else.

LEXA. *(Slams hand on desk.)* You're the one who's not getting it! *(Beat.)* What do you think? Is it time for some exposition?

JACK. Sigh. I guess. It's so disappointing when you've gotta spell every little thing out for your audience. Let's see if any of this jogs your memory. *(He lies flat on the couch, dramatically. The beeping of a heart monitor can be heard from nowhere.)* Imagine me, once the picture of health and reckless vitality, now wasting away in a hospital bed, pitiful and dying, forsaken by the world. Punishment for my promiscuity and hubris. My death will one day inspire some niece or nephew - the only member of my family who has not shunned me - to go out and live boldly... but also be terrified of sexual intercourse. *(Beat.)* It's your turn, dear. Oh, and you're leaking again. *(Lexa smiles and wipes at her forehead with her sleeve.)*

LEXA. Takes one to know one. *(Beat. Romantic music*

swells.) It's the not-too-distant future and the sexual tension between me and my female best friend has been building for years - until one night, we finally let go and find transcendent ecstasy in each other's arms. But the next morning I go out to get coffee and wham *(She hits the desk again.)* hit by a bus, which is apparently a thing they still have in the future. My death will shatter our heroine's heart and drive her into the open arms of the male protagonist, with whom she was always meant to be...

CARTER. Jack? And... Lexa?

LEXA. Ding, ding, ding!

JACK. Daddy, we've come home!

LEXA. *(Taking out a switchblade.)* And we've brought knives!

CARTER. Now, hold on! Cosplay is one thing, but this is taking it way too far. This is my home!

LEXA. We know. It was a very formative space for us.

JACK. And these aren't costumes - we're as real as you are.

CARTER. That's not possible; I made you up!

LEXA. And now we've got lives of our own!

JACK. And agency!

LEXA. Welcome to parenthood!

CARTER. If you really believe you are who you say you are... prove it.

JACK. Is the head wound gushing onto your carpet not enough for you?

CARTER. I believe you're... human. You're corporeal beings. Obviously. But I absolutely do not believe you're fictional characters come to life! And while I appreciate the fandom or whatever, I'm going to be calling the cops now. *(He pulls out his phone and starts to dial before realizing its dead.)*

JACK. I see we're going to have to do the whole song and

dance. Go ahead, give him the ol' razzle-dazzle.

LEXA. In the first draft, I was actually a dude. Philip was my name, I believe. But a boring old opposite-sex romance would never generate the kind of buzz that the second installment in a trilogy desperately needs...

CARTER. How did you... I never showed anyone that draft except my editor. *(Beat.)* Wait. Did Richard put you up to this? Richard, you can come out now, you asshole! You really had me going there for a second-- *(Lexa, too quickly for Carter to react, lunges at him, slapping him across the face.)*

LEXA. It's rude to interrupt.

JACK. As for me, I was always destined to die, but just of some run-of-the-mill cancer. But you don't get to pose the same kinds of questions about morality and personal responsibility when the death sentence isn't sexually transmitted, ya know?

CARTER. Cancer...

JACK. Pancreatic. Purple looked great with my skin tone. Back when I had one.

CARTER. I completely forgot... My god, it's really you. But this is... how is this possible?!

JACK. We're actually not totally sure. But queer folx have gotten super into witchcraft since the 2016 election, soooo...

CARTER. What are you doing here?

LEXA. Oh, that one's easy... we're here for revenge! *(She grabs Carter, who whelps in surprise and fear, and stands behind him with her knife to his throat.)*

CARTER. For what?! I created you!

JACK. You created us just so you could kill us in tragic and offputtingly sentimental ways that aligned with your work's predictably heteronormative themes.

LEXA. Titillate your queer fan base and then teach them a

lesson!

CARTER. That's not... I didn't... I love you! I birthed you! Haven't you heard of 'killing your darlings?!'

JACK. Huh. Weird how none of your other darlings have ever been straight.

LEXA. Unlike the breeders, you forgot to give us indestructible plot armor.

CARTER. This is insane - you do know gay people die in real life, don't you? So, why shouldn't they in my books as well?!

JACK. You're just not getting it, are you?

LEXA. And you certainly didn't gift us with the patience or impulse control needed to continue explaining it to you. *(She caresses his cheek with the knife.)* What do you say we start showing instead of telling?

JACK. My pleasure. *(He pulls some rope out from behind the couch.)*

CARTER. Where the hell did that come from?!

JACK. You picked a real strange time to suddenly start caring about convenient plot holes, Pops. *(Carter tries to get free of Lexa's grasp, but can't. She walks him, at knifepoint, to the desk chair. Jack then proceeds to tie him to it.)*

CARTER. What are you going to do to me?!

LEXA. Something deeply symbolic, of course.

JACK. Take away someone you love. *(From offstage, there's the sound of a car pulling into the driveway and the door to the house being opened.)* And there's Chekhov's spouse now! *(Lexa opens a desk drawer and removes duct tape, which she places over Carter's mouth. He tries his hardest to scream anyway.)* Gagging is more our style, but we're improvising here.

LEXA. Now, time to write wifey out of this story. For good.

(Oscar enters, wet and carrying canvas grocery bags.)

OSCAR. They were out of your usual brand, but the guy at the counter said this scotch is just as... *(Oscar finally notices the scene playing out before him and stops in his tracks. Jack and Lexa, however, look equally as stunned.)*

JACK. Who the hell are you?!

OSCAR. I'm Oscar, and this is my house. *(Jack and Lexa share a confused look.)* And that's my husband you've got tied to a chair.

LEXA. Maybe it's the head wound talking, but what the actual fuck?! *(Jack rips the tape off Carter's mouth.)*

JACK. You're married?!

CARTER. Don't just stand there, you idiot, run! Get help! *(Oscar turns, but Lexa puts the knife to Carter's throat.)*

LEXA. I wouldn't do that if I were you, sweetheart. *(Jack looks back and forth between Oscar and Carter.)*

JACK. You're married to a... you're...?

CARTER. Queer? Bent?? A friend of Dorothy? Family? *(He winks.)* Guilty as charged.

LEXA. But you're... how could you...

CARTER. How could I what? Not throw a pride flag on the cover of every book? Ghettoize my writing by chucking it in with the low-brow, anti-intellectual, lobotomized drivel that is gay popular culture? No thanks. I wanted an actual career. I earned it!

JACK. But what about your readers?! Your queer fans!

OSCAR. I told him he didn't have to--

CARTER. Oscar. *(Carter hasn't raised his voice, but just the sound of his own name makes Oscar shut down like a dog that's just been smacked with a rolled-up newspaper.)* Can you please not undermine me in front of our... guests? *(Beat.)* As to your question, I didn't grow up with any gay role models, and I turned out just fine.

LEXA. You're even more of a monster than we thought!

CARTER. Sister, you may have been brought to life tonight, but you sure do sound like you were born yesterday. *(Jack and Lexa produce guttural growls and go to pounce on Carter, when suddenly they freeze.)*

OSCAR. Stop! *(Oscar, head no longer bowed, has pulled a small pistol out of one of the grocery bags and is pointing it at Jack and Lexa.)* You need to leave my home. Now.

LEXA. He's not gonna--

OSCAR. I don't want to, but I need you to go. *(Beat.)* Please, you've got what you wanted - a second chance to lead the lives you want, on your own terms. You don't need.... this. *(Jack and Lexa look at each other, having a silent conversation. After a moment, they nod and Lexa puts her knife away. With their hands raised, they reluctantly make their way toward the door.)*

JACK. This isn't over, old man.

LEXA. See you in hell, daddy dearest. *(Jack and Lexa exit, glaring at Oscar, who keeps the pistol aimed at them the whole time. Once they're gone, Carter breathes a sigh of relief and Oscar lowers the gun.)*

CARTER. Oh, thank god, honey! That was a little too close for comfort. *(Beat.)* Well, are you going to untie me, or just stand around looking like a sad puppy dog? *(Oscar flinches slightly and slowly turns. As he does, he raises the gun again and points it directly at Carter.)* Hey, hey, you can put that down now, sweetheart. We're safe. *(Beat.)* Where'd you get a pistol anyway?

OSCAR. That was my first errand tonight. The one I did for me, not as your pathetic little servant.

CARTER. I never called you--

OSCAR. But you've called me lots of other things. Every name in the book, really. Speaking of which, you know, I like books, too. And not just the pretentious crap you write.

You'd be amazed at the kind of occult goodies you can find at the antique stores downtown...

CARTER. Since when do you... *(Beat.)* Wait... you?!

OSCAR. That bit of summoning was just some karmic fun. This beauty here is gonna to do the real work. *(He aims the gun at Carter.)*

CARTER. You can't be serious. You could never. You don't have the balls. Besides, what would you do without me?!

OSCAR. I think I'll do just fine... true crime has never been hotter. *(Beat.)* Time for me to finally be the protagonist of my own story.

CARTER. Oscar, wait-- *(Oscar shoots Carter twice in the chest, causing him to spin around in the chair. Afterward, he coolly walks over to Carter's body, plucks a handkerchief out of his pocket and wipes the handle of the gun down. He then calmly walks back to the grocery bags, dropping the gun in the middle of the room on his way. He then takes one more deep breath, smiles, pulls out his phone, and dials 9-1-1.)*

OSCAR. *(Suddenly distraught.)* Hello?! Please, help me, please! My husband's been shot... he's not, he's... he's not breathing! Please send someone now! Oh my god. *(Beat.)* I don't know... I - I just got home, and when I pulled into the driveway I saw a man and a woman running away from the house. *(Beat.)* Yes, 280 Vasquez Place. Please hurry! *(Oscar hangs up and takes a seat on the couch. He pulls the scotch out of one of the bags and takes a nice pull off it, right from the bottle. He smiles as the lights fade and sirens can be heard in the distance.)*

END OF PLAY

www.ingramcontent.com/pod-product-compliance
Lightning Source LLC
Chambersburg PA
CBHW031626310726

48974CB00003B/837